Unicorn Academy
...Where magic happens!

Phoebe and Shimmer

JULIE
SYKES

illustrated by
LUCY
TRUMAN

nosy
crow

For Hettie and Maddie, who love magic.
May you always believe in fairies
and unicorns.

First published in the UK in 2020 by Nosy Crow Ltd
The Crow's Nest, 14 Baden Place
Crosby Row, London, SE1 1YW

www.nosycrow.com

ISBN: 978 1 78800 926 3

Nosy Crow and associated logos are trademarks
and/or registered trademarks of Nosy Crow Ltd.

Text copyright © Julie Sykes and Linda Chapman, 2020
Illustrations copyright © Lucy Truman, 2020
Cover typography © Joel Holland, 2020

A CIP catalogue record for this book is available from the British Library.

Printed and bound in Great Britain by Clays Ltd, Elcograf S.p.A.

Papers used by Nosy Crow are made from
wood grown in sustainable forests.

MIX
Paper from
responsible sources
FSC® C018072
www.fsc.org

1 3 5 7 9 10 8 6 4 2

CHAPTER ONE

"You'll never guess what I just saw!" Phoebe exclaimed, bursting into Amethyst dorm. Her eyes sparkled with excitement. "Well?" she said, looking round eagerly at her dorm mates – Zara, Lily and Aisha. "Come on, guess!"

"No time. You can tell us later," said Zara, pulling her hoodie over her dark-brown hair.

"Yes, hurry up now, Phoebs, or we'll be late for the cross-country ride with Ms Tulip," said Lily. Aisha didn't say anything, she was too busy rummaging under her bed.

"But this is important!" Phoebe protested. She

wanted her friends to feel the same excitement she did. "OK, so this is what happened," she said, going into what Zara teasingly called her "story-telling mode". "I was coming back from breakfast, just walking along the corridor, minding my own business when I saw Ms Rosemary and Ms Rivers whispering together outside Ms Nettles' office. They left and I heard Ms Nettles making a weird noise so I sneaked a look around the door and guess what?" Phoebe paused dramatically as she remembered what she had seen in the headteacher's office. "Ms Nettles was looking really upset and dabbing at her eyes!"

Her friends continued to get

ready, not taking much notice.

"She was crying!" Phoebe exaggerated, to get their attention. "Loudly, with lots of tears. Well, what do you think about that?"

"Found it!" Aisha's bottom, followed by the rest of her, appeared backwards from under her bed. She was clutching a purple hoodie. "Who was sighing?"

"Ms Nettles was *crying*," said Phoebe, looking round at her friends in exasperation. "Don't you think that was super weird? Headteachers don't cry. Something must be going on!"

"The thing is, was Ms Nettles really crying, Phoebe?" Zara said, giving her a doubtful look. "Or are you just exaggerating like usual?"

"No! I'm not!" Phoebe insisted. "I promise, Ms Nettles was a hundred per cent crying. She blew her nose and it sounded as loud as an elephant trumpeting!"

"Oh dear, I hope she's OK," said Lily, looking concerned.

Zara frowned. "I'm sure she is. There's probably a simple explanation. Her eyes could have been streaming because her hay fever was playing up."

Phoebe rolled her eyes. "You are *so* boring, Zara!"

"Not boring, just sensible," said Zara, with a grin. "Seriously, there's been enough drama happening here without having to make stuff up, Phoebs. Purple tornadoes sweeping across the island, the school almost being destroyed, a strange voice in the tornado saying they're not going to be stopped…"

"Aha! But maybe those things have got something to do with Ms Nettles crying," said Phoebe triumphantly. "Maybe something else has happened and she's just found out about it – maybe there's been another tornado or something

even –" she paused dramatically – *"worse!"*

"Or maybe Ms Nettles just has hay fever," said Zara again. "It is springtime after all, and there's a lot of pollen in the air."

Lily threw Phoebe's hoodie at her. "Come on, Phoebs. We really have to go. We'll be in trouble with Ms Tulip if we're late."

Phoebe sighed as she pulled her purple hoodie on. She brushed her long honey-blonde hair before braiding it into plaits. She loved her three friends in Amethyst dorm but she sometimes felt they really didn't get her. She liked to make everything that happened seem as exciting as possible but they seemed to just want to know the bare truth. How boring was that?

Shimmer will want to hear about Ms Nettles, she comforted herself as she got ready. A warm glow spread through her as she thought of her handsome unicorn. Shimmer loved drama and

5

storytelling just as much as she did. *He's the best,* Phoebe thought happily as she followed the others to the stable block. *I'm so glad Ms Nettles paired me with him.*

She'd never forget that first day at Unicorn Academy – arriving at the school and seeing the beautiful glass-and-marble building glittering in the sunlight, meeting the rest of her dorm and being paired with her own perfect unicorn. Students arrived at the academy in the January when they were ten, and stayed a whole year. During that year, they got to know their unicorn partner and learned all about Unicorn Island so that they could become the guardians of it when they were older.

"Look at all the flowers," said Lily as they made their way across the lawn. She pointed to the beds of bright spring bulbs – tulips, bluebells and a huge swathe of daffodils waving their yellow heads in

the morning breeze. "Aren't they beautiful?"

Phoebe stooped to pick a daffodil, thinking that it would look nice in her hair. She froze as she heard an angry shout.

"Stop right there!" It was Ms Bramble, the head gardener. She stomped over with a rake in her hand. "I hope you weren't about to pick a daffodil."

"Definitely not. I would never do that, Ms Bramble." Phoebe shook her head emphatically and tried to look as innocent as possible. "Flowers should be left in the ground for everyone to enjoy. I was just bending over to … to smell them."

Ms Bramble gave her a suspicious look. "Hmm. Very well. Hurry along then. You're crushing the grass!"

"Yes, Ms Bramble," said Phoebe politely, wondering why the gardener was being quite so grumpy. People often picked the daffodils. There

were hundreds of them.

As she ran after her friends, she mimicked Ms Bramble's expression: first cross then suspicious. Phoebe loved watching people so that she could imitate them later. Her old drama teacher had taught her that to make acting come alive you had to draw on real life experiences. "Hurry along now, girls! You're crushing the grass!" she said, wagging her finger at her friends and mimicking Ms Bramble's voice.

They giggled and continued on to the stables.

Shimmer whinnied when he saw Phoebe. He was a tall unicorn with a long pink-and-pale blue mane that fell over his deep-brown eyes. His thick tail flowed to the ground like a waterfall. "Are you looking forward to going around the cross-country course, Phoebe?" he said eagerly. "Is it a race this time? I bet we can win if it is. I can jump really high and I'm faster than all the other unicorns!"

"I know you are," said Phoebe proudly. She brushed Shimmer's coat then carefully combed out the tangles in his mane and tail. As she worked she told him about the teachers and their strange behaviour.

"*No! Really?*" he exclaimed, opening his eyes wide. "Ms Brambles *bellowed* at you and you saw Ms Nettles *sobbing* on the floor! That's dreadful. I'll ask the other unicorns if they know anything about it."

"Yes, do that!" said Phoebe, happy that at least Shimmer had a satisfying reaction to her news. "The others think I'm exaggerating but I'm absolutely *sure* something is going on."

They went out into the yard where a noisy group of students and unicorns was gathering. Amethyst dorm shared their riding lessons with the students from Opal and Topaz dorms. Ms Tulip was late arriving. She was small, pretty and energetic and her lessons were always a lot of fun, but today she seemed unusually flustered.

"It's bad news, I'm afraid," she said, clapping her hands for silence. "The cross-country ride is cancelled. Ms Nettles has asked that we tidy the stables and yard instead. Everything has to look as neat and shiny as a new hoof pick. I'm sorry," she added, raising her hands to silence the groans.

"Can't we just have a quick ride over a few jumps? You know we'll work harder if we can

do some jumping first," Spike from Topaz dorm pleaded, leading a chorus of, "Go on, Ms Tulip. Pleeeeeease say yes."

Ms Tulip shook her head. "Unicorn Academy is being inspected, but if there's enough time you can go for a quick ride once everywhere is tidy."

Phoebe gasped. "Are they thinking of shutting the school down?"

"Of course not, Phoebe," said Ms Tulip. "It's just an inspection but naturally Ms Nettles and all of the staff want to show the academy off to its best and highlight all the wonderful things we do here. So, let's get started. Topaz dorm, you can tidy the yard, Opal, the storeroom, and Amethyst, the big barn next door. When you've finished, you can head out for a ride in your dorm groups but no jumping without me, remember."

Phoebe was intrigued. "I absolutely bet this inspection was the reason Ms Nettles was crying

earlier!" she hissed to Zara, Lily and Aisha, as their unicorns went sadly back to their stables to wait for them, and they trooped to the barn to start tidying. "Do you think she's in trouble because she and the teachers left us here alone when that purple tornado almost hit the school?"

"Possibly," said Zara, thoughtfully. "It was a really dangerous situation."

"The school could have been destroyed if Feather hadn't discovered her moving magic in time and diverted the tornado out to sea where it wouldn't harm anyone," said Aisha. She smiled at Lily. "You and Feather were brilliant. Her magic is awesome."

Lily blushed. "Thanks." None of the Amethyst dorm unicorns had discovered their magic yet except for Feather. Each young unicorn at the academy had a special power. Some, like Feather, discovered theirs quickly, while others took longer.

Phoebe and Shimmer

Those unicorns who hadn't found their magic, or bonded with their partner, by the end of the first year had to stay on at Unicorn Academy for a second year.

Phoebe hoped that Shimmer would find his magic very soon. She wanted it to be something amazing, that would make everyone gaze in wonder – maybe light magic so he could create rainbows, or flying magic. She also couldn't wait for them to bond. When it happened, a strand of her long hair would turn the same pink and blue as Shimmer's mane to show everyone they were partners for life. How cool would that be?

"I'm glad there haven't been any more tornadoes," said Aisha, with a shiver.

"It is strange the culprit's never been caught," said Zara.

Phoebe stopped with a gasp. "That's it!" she exclaimed, throwing her hands up in the air. "I

bet *that's* why Ms Nettles was crying!"

"Why?' said Lily, looking puzzled.

"Because people suspect she is the culprit!" Phoebe said dramatically. "Don't you see? This inspection is happening because people think *Ms Nettles* is to blame!"

CHAPTER TWO

"Phoebe!" Zara was shocked. "You can't go around saying stuff like that without any evidence to back it up."

"You really can't," agreed Lily quickly. "Ms Nettles loves the school. She'd never hurt it."

"Aha, but maybe she's just pretending to love it," said Phoebe, excitedly. "Remember that a couple of years ago the headteacher before Ms Nettles did all sorts of things to try to harm the academy. Maybe Ms Nettles has turned *evil* just like her!"

"No, no, no!" protested Aisha, looking shocked.

"Ms Nettles isn't evil!"

Phoebe raised her eyebrows and folded her arms. "She might be."

"Phoebe, it really can't be Ms Nettles," said Zara sensibly. "We know the person responsible for the tornadoes is a man.

Remember how we heard him shouting when Feather moved the tornado away from the academy. He said: *'You think you can stop me but you can't.'*"

"Oh, yes," said Phoebe, her excitement subsiding.

"I guess that Ms Nettles might be upset because she's worried about the inspection," said Zara. "If she really

was crying this morning like you say then that may have been why."

"We should make sure the inspector thinks the school is perfect!" said Lily. "I don't want Ms Nettles to get into trouble."

"Me neither," said Aisha. "Let's talk to the inspector and tell them how brilliant all the teachers are – and what a great headteacher Ms Nettles is."

"Definitely!" agreed Zara.

They reached the messy barn. A few of the hay bales inside it had burst and there was hay all over the floor.

"Oh dear, we'd better get some brooms and start sweeping," said Aisha with a sigh.

"This will take ages," grumbled Phoebe.

Lily grinned. "Not if we use magic! Wait here, I'll go and get Feather!"

Feather's moving magic was very useful when

it came to tidying up. Soon the barn was filled with the sweet scent of burnt sugar – the smell of unicorn magic. Pink sparkles were fading in the air, the loose hay was all in one big tidy pile and the other hay bales were piled up neatly.

"There!" said Feather happily.

"You're the best!" said Lily, hugging her. The yellow, violet and blue streak in her dark hair merged with Feather's mane.

Phoebe felt a flicker of envy. She really hoped she and Shimmer would bond soon. She could just imagine everyone fussing around them and praising them. It would be fantastic!

With the barn tidy, Amethyst dorm set out for a ride around the grounds, sticking to the meadow to avoid the cross-country course. They cantered through the wildflowers and then let their unicorns splash in the sparkling stream.

As they rode back towards the stable yard they

saw a man in a suit getting out of a horse-drawn carriage at the school entrance. He was tall and thin with a severe face.

"Who's that?" said Aisha.

"I bet it's the inspector!" said Zara.

"But Ms Tulip said he wouldn't be here until tomorrow," said Lily.

"I know but it's got to be him. Look at the clues. He's carrying a suitcase and a clipboard just like an inspector would, he's wearing a suit which means he's someone who's here on formal business, and he's arrived in a carriage which only someone official would do," said Zara.

"And he's already being nosey," said Phoebe, as the man peered at the fountain in front of the school, frowned, and noted something on his clipboard. "I wonder if Ms Tulip knows he's here already."

"We should warn her!" said Zara.

They set off at a canter. When they reached the stables and told Ms Tulip about the man, she looked worried. "Oh dear. It does sound like the inspector has arrived early. I hope he doesn't come out here yet. We've not finished tidying."

"Don't worry. Feather will help!" said Lily.

Feather nodded eagerly.

While Feather used her magic to help finish the tidying, the rest of the students quickly groomed their unicorns to make them look smart, and sorted out their stables so the straw beds were clean and fluffy and the haynets full.

Ms Tulip gave a sigh of relief as she looked around the gleaming yard. "Well done, everyone, I think we're finally ready. Feather, you deserve a huge bucket of sky berries. Thank you! You must be tired out after using so much magic."

Lily fetched Feather a bucket of the sweet juicy berries that grew behind the school. Sky berries

were unicorns' favourite food, and they were full of the vitamins they needed to stay healthy and keep their magic strong. Then, leaving the unicorns to rest, the girls went in for lunch.

The students were tucking into delicious baked potatoes with melted cheese and salad when Ms Nettles showed the stranger into the dining room. Clapping her hands for silence, she introduced him.

"This is Mr Longnose, everyone. He will be with us for a few days and is here to inspect the school. He will be sitting in on your lessons and he may want to ask you some questions. I hope you will all be very helpful and answer to the best of your ability."

Phoebe studied Mr Longnose. With his dark suit, black tie, shiny black shoes and sharp eyes, he looked like a perfect villain. "I don't like him,"

she hissed to the others as Ms Nettles and Mr Longnose sat down together and the students started talking again. "He looks shifty to me!"

"Me too," Aisha agreed.

Phoebe gave the inspector a suspicious look. "I think he's up to something."

"Yes, inspecting the school!" said Zara, rolling her eyes. "Honestly, Phoebe. Next you'll be imagining *he* was responsible for the tornadoes!"

Phoebe fell silent but watched the inspector carefully for the rest of lunch.

Afterwards, they had a Geography class with Ms Rivers. When they arrived at their classroom with Opal and Topaz dorms, they found Mr Longnose already at the back of the room with his clipboard and an array of pens set out neatly on the desk before him.

"Good afternoon." His voice was clipped.

"Good afternoon," everyone said politely.

Exchanging looks, they all sat down.

The inspector walked over to Phoebe and Zara's desk. "Do you like being here at the academy?" he asked Phoebe.

"Oh yes, I love it!" Phoebe said eagerly, keen to tell him how amazing the academy was. "It's the most exciting place!"

The inspector frowned. "Exciting?"

"Yes, there's always some huge drama happening!" Phoebe felt Zara kick her sharply under the desk and glanced at her. Zara was looking panicked and giving tiny but frantic shakes of her head.

"Drama?" the inspector echoed, his frown deepening. "So, you don't feel safe here?"

Phoebe's eyes widened. She hadn't meant that at all. "No, no, that isn't what—"

Just then, Ms Rivers walked in.

"Quiet please!" their teacher said, cutting

across Phoebe's words.

"*Students don't feel safe,*" the inspector muttered under his breath, making a note on his clipboard as he went back to his seat.

"Phoebe, you doughnut!" Zara hissed in horror. "Why did you say that?"

Phoebe felt awful. She hadn't meant to give the impression that the students felt unsafe. Oh, why hadn't she thought more carefully about what she was saying? What if Ms Nettles got into trouble because of her?

I'll try and to talk to him later, she thought, glancing back at the inspector, who was still scribbling notes. *I'll make sure he knows I didn't mean it and that I think the academy is the best school ever!*

CHAPTER THREE

"Today we are going to be studying the thermal springs in the west of the island," Ms Rivers announced. "They are in a mountainous landscape that is home to the golden-spotted phoenix."

There was the clatter of chair legs on the floor and Mr Longnose stood up. "Excuse me, Ms Rivers, but I am a trained geologist. I happen to have visited the thermal springs. Would you like me to share some of my knowledge with the class?"

"Certainly," said Ms Rivers politely. "I'm sure they'll all be very interested in what you have to say."

"Oh, we will! We really will!" Phoebe burst out, hoping to make up for her earlier mistake by letting the inspector see how enthusiastic they all were about learning.

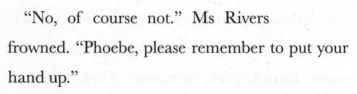

"Ms Rivers, is it usual for pupils to be allowed to shout out in your class?" enquired Mr Longnose sharply.

"No, of course not." Ms Rivers frowned. "Phoebe, please remember to put your hand up."

Phoebe slid back into her seat. Flapdoodles! She hadn't made things better, if anything she'd made them worse!

Mr Longnose launched into a long and boring

description of how the hot springs were formed and then showed them how to greet the golden-spotted phoenix. "It's polite to bow from the waist like so, while extending your right hand out at exactly this angle."

Phoebe heard Spike and his friend Johan swallow snorts of laugher as Mr Longnose folded his thin frame in half while twisting his wrist to hold out his hand with the fingers making a circle.

Mr Longnose looked up sharply. "How rude!" he said in a displeased voice. "I am surprised you allow behaviour like this, Ms Rivers." Picking up his clipboard, he made another note.

Ms Rivers fixed the boys with a look that made them subside instantly. "Thank you, Mr Longnose, for all that information. It's been most enlightening." Although her words were polite, Phoebe could tell from the tightness around her mouth and eyes that she was not happy at all.

When Geography ended, they went to get a snack in the dining hall before going to a library session with Ms Tansy, the librarian. Mr Longnose walked to the hall with them, asking questions of everyone as they went. Did they like the school? Did they feel safe?

"I'm going to talk to him," Phoebe told Zara.

"No, Phoebs!" Zara grabbed her arm.

Phoebe frowned. "Why not? I just want to make sure he knows students don't feel unsafe here and to tell him how utterly amazing the school is."

"Please, don't," Zara begged. "You never think before you speak and you'll only make things worse." She sounded so genuinely worried that Phoebe was taken aback. She and Zara often teased each other – she would tell Zara she was too sensible and Zara would tell her she was too dramatic – but this time Zara didn't sound as if she was teasing.

"Come on, let's get rainbow cakes," said Zara, pulling her into the dining hall.

Phoebe followed her, feeling confused and hurt. Did Zara really think she would make things worse if she spoke to the inspector?

"Where are the cakes today?" asked Aisha as they got to the counter.

"Didn't you hear?" said Lauren, from Opal dorm. "The kitchen ran out of flour. The delivery didn't get through because Mount Inferno started rumbling overnight, and the main road to the north has been closed while scientists investigate whether it's going to erupt."

"Really?" said Zara in surprise. As she loved science, she often read reports about the ancient volcano in the mountains behind the school. "But Mount Inferno has been dormant for over a hundred years."

"I overheard Ms Rivers and Ms Nettles talking

about it at lunchtime," said Spike, joining in the conversation. "No one knows why it's suddenly active again."

"Luckily no one lives on its slopes," said Zara. "And school's far enough away to be out of the reach of the lava if it does erupt. The big danger will be to the villages nearby on the coast. Volcanic activity can affect the tides and Mount Inferno is covered by a glacier – a massive river of ice. If it does erupt, the glacier will melt which will cause dreadful flooding."

"I hope it doesn't erupt!" said Lily anxiously.

"Maybe it's just going to rumble for a bit," said Aisha.

As everyone continued talking about the volcano, Zara shot Phoebe a puzzled look. "You're being quiet."

"Am I?"

"Yes, normally if you heard news like this, you'd

be waving your arms, telling us we're all going to die!"

"Ha ha!" said Phoebe. "Very funny." But she didn't really feel like laughing for once. Zara's words from before were still stinging. While the others carried on talking about the volcano, she slipped away and went to the stables.

Shimmer whickered when he saw her. "Phoebe!"

"Hi, Shimmer," Phoebe muttered.

He blinked. "Are you OK?"

Phoebe shrugged.

"You're obviously not. What's the matter?" he asked, nuzzling her hands.

She sighed. "Do you think I'm a doughnut?"

"What? No! Of course not!" Shimmer looked confused. "What are you talking about?"

Phoebe put her arms round his neck and told him what had happened. "Zara said I'd make

things worse if I spoke to the inspector. Would I have made it worse, Shimmer?"

"No, of course not," Shimmer said loyally. He blew gently on her face. "You always say the right thing. You're perfect."

Phoebe loved him for being so supportive but a tiny little bit of her brain did wonder if Zara might be right. She sighed. "Maybe I do need to think more before I speak and not exaggerate as much," she said. "I did give the inspector the wrong idea."

"No!" said Shimmer quickly. "Now, you *are* being a doughnut! Please don't change. I like you just the way you are."

Phoebe smiled. "Thanks, Shimmer." She was very lucky to have him. He understood her in a way that no one else did. "I'd better go back in. We've got a library session now and no doubt Mr Long-*Nosey* will be asking lots more questions. I

don't like him. I hope he doesn't write a really bad report on the school." She caught her breath. "What if he does and Ms Nettles loses her job? Or what if it's so bad, the school is shut down and we're all sent home *for ever?*"

Shimmer whickered as if he was laughing. "That's more like it!" He nudged her. "But even I think you're exaggerating now. Everyone knows how brilliant Unicorn Academy is. One bad report won't be enough to close it."

Phoebe really hoped he was right.

CHAPTER FOUR

Ms Tansy gathered them all together around the reading tree – a giant tree that grew through the floor of the library. She seemed nervous to have Mr Longnose in the lesson with her and fiddled with her flowery, yellow-framed glasses. "Right. Today, everyone, we're going to practise your researching skills by looking up famous inventors. I want you to start by trying to find out about Count Lysander Thornberry."

"I shall be fascinated to see what you find in books," Mr Longnose said. "I know the count personally. He is a first-rate scientist and an

exceptional inventor. He was the first person to successfully combine magic and science to make a rain machine." A disapproving look crossed his face. "He might be vain with a ridiculously flamboyant dress sense but his work is undeniably brilliant."

Zara put her hand up. "I thought the count was a recluse and avoided people." She loved science and often read science books and magazines for fun. "How do you know him, Mr Longnose?"

"We studied geology together before he became famous," said Mr Longnose, with a sniff. "The count was lucky enough to continue with his scientific work, becoming the famous inventor everyone knows today, whereas I had to give up my research and get a paid job."

Phoebe raised her hand. "Mr Longnose, if you studied geology, do you know much about volcanoes?"

"Phoebe, that's really not relevant," said Ms Tansy, giving the inspector an anxious glance. "Today's lesson is about inventors not volcanoes."

"No, no, it is quite all right, Ms Tansy," said Mr Longnose, his expression losing some of its usual severity. "Volcanoes are a particular interest of mine and I completed several research papers on them before I became a school inspector. Do you have a question about volcanoes?" he asked Phoebe.

Phoebe nodded. "We heard that Mount Inferno's rumbling. How likely is it to erupt?"

"Now *that* is a very interesting question," Mr Longnose said. He steepled his fingers beneath his chin. "Dormant volcanoes sometimes start to show signs of activity without erupting. The rumblings from Mount Inferno may be false alarms or they may signal that an eruption is imminent."

"Will we be in danger here if it does erupt?" Tom from Topaz dorm asked.

"No, although the effects will be felt elsewhere – most particularly on the coast. A serious eruption will cause all sorts of problems." Mr Longnose looked strangely excited. "If it does happen, it will be a most interesting event to study. Most interesting indeed!"

Phoebe watched his face curiously. He looked almost as if he *wanted* it to happen!

"Now, any other questions?" he asked.

"Why do you think it has become active again after all these years?" asked Zara.

"Well, there are several possibilities." Mr Longnose launched into a long rambling speech about dormant volcanoes.

Zara listened carefully but Phoebe soon gave up paying attention. Her thoughts returned to earlier. Despite Shimmer urging her not to change, she

wondered if she should try not to exaggerate so much. It was much more fun to make dull events into exciting stories but she still felt bad she'd given Mr Longnose the wrong impression of the school, and she disliked the way Zara hadn't trusted her to put things right. She sighed. Maybe she should stick to the truth more.

You know what, I'll try, she decided.

Phoebe's decision was quickly put to the test. As the day went on, more and more reports started coming in about the rumbling Mount Inferno. It appeared there had been several mini eruptions which were already causing problems.

"I spoke to my aunt and she said there was such a high tide this afternoon a rainbow-fountain whale got beached on the roof of her house," Spike said at dinner.

"And apparently the village next to ours has

fallen down a huge crack that opened up in the road," countered Johan.

"And Lauren said that her cousin's house was under—" Phoebe broke off. She'd been about to say *underwater*. But really all Lauren had told her was that her cousin's family were evacuating from their village because of the potential risk of flooding. She sighed as she decided not to add to the story. Being truthful was very boring.

"Under what?" said Zara.

"Nothing," muttered Phoebe, but as she saw everyone lose interest in her and start to look away, she suddenly couldn't resist. "Well, she said it was under a whole *sea* of water!" she said, her eyes widening. "Her family lost everything – clothes, furniture, even the walls of the house were knocked down!"

She felt a rush of satisfaction as the others listened eagerly. Adding to the facts was so much

more fun than sticking to them!

Ms Nettles rose to her feet and waited until silence descended in the room. "Students, I need to talk to you about Mount Inferno. I believe that you have heard that it has recently reawakened but I want to assure you that help is being sent to those in need and you will be quite safe here at the academy."

Mr Longnose unfolded his long legs and stood up beside her. "Quite right, Ms Nettles. There is nothing to worry about. However, this event is a once-in-a-lifetime occurrence, and for that reason I propose that the students should go on a scientific expedition to the coast. They can study the effects of the volcano becoming active again after so long."

Ms Nettles blinked, looking taken aback. "A field trip? But Mr Longnose, I cannot just interrupt the curriculum to let the students go off camping."

"Why not?" said Mr Longnose, looking surprised. "It will help further their understanding of the island. I will choose an area I believe to be free from the risk of serious flooding but somewhere they will be able to observe the effects of an active volcano at first hand. I suggest they measure both frequency and strength of earth tremors while at the same time recording the sea levels at high and low tide. I will, of course, be happy to accompany them and share my extensive knowledge of volcanoes."

For once, Ms Nettles seemed lost for words. "I don't think this is a good idea, Mr Longnose."

Mr Longnose's eyebrows raised. "I'm sorry, Ms Nettles? Are you saying you do not believe it is a good idea for your students to make the most of an exciting educational opportunity?"

"Of course not!" said Ms Nettles, unusually ruffled.

"Good," Mr Longnose interrupted. "Then the field trip will take place. We leave tomorrow."

He sat back down and picked up his knife and fork.

Ms Nettles took a deep breath, and then looked round at the agog students. "It appears there will be a field trip, after all," she said abruptly. "Lessons will be cancelled to allow everyone to get ready. You can collect the food and camping equipment needed for yourselves and your unicorns after breakfast tomorrow."

The students broke into excited chatter as Ms Nettles sat back down.

"A camping trip instead of lessons!" said Phoebe. "How awesome!"

"I wish we didn't have Mr Longnose tagging along though," said Lily. "I hate the way he keeps asking questions. It's like he only wants to find bad things out about the school."

"Let's stay out of his way," said Phoebe. "Just think – sleeping in tents, toasting marshmallows on the campfire." Her eyes shone. "And telling ghost stories at night!"

"I'll pack a flute so we can have some music," said Aisha enthusiastically. "Not my best one though in case it gets sandy."

"Studying the earth tremors and tide levels will be so interesting," said Zara excitedly. "I'll get some books on volcanoes from the library to read while we're there."

Phoebe rolled her eyes. "You *really* know how to have fun."

"It *is* fun," said Zara.

"You're nuttier than a squirrel!" Phoebe told her.

Zara grinned. "You can talk! I'm also going to bring my detective notebook in case there's more to Mount Inferno coming to life than meets the eye."

"What do you mean?" asked Aisha, frowning.

Zara lowered her voice. "Don't you lot think it's odd that two really unusual environmental things happen within a few months of each other? First, the purple tornadoes and now this. We know the tornadoes were caused by someone using bad magic. Maybe that same person has caused Mount Inferno to become active in order to harm the island some more."

"You really think they might be linked?" breathed Lily.

Zara nodded. "My uncle, the one who's

a detective, says you should be very wary of coincidences. We should look out for clues, see if there are any links between the two events while we're on the coast. Are you all in? Will you help me try to solve this mystery?"

"Definitely!" Phoebe, Lily and Aisha chorused.

Phoebe felt excitement tingle through her. The field trip had suddenly got even more fun!

CHAPTER FIVE

The next morning, Ms Nettles announced that the whole school was going to be allowed to travel to the coast using the magic map to save time. Everyone was very excited – the map was an exact model of the island that stood in the assembly hall and could be used to take people and their unicorns anywhere on the island they wanted to go.

Seated on their unicorns, Phoebe, Zara, Aisha and Lily gathered around the map with the rest of the school. Their rucksacks were filled with camping equipment. Zara's was heavier than

everyone else's because she seemed to have packed half the library!

Phoebe felt like she was going to explode with excitement. "This is so awesome!" she exclaimed. "I can't wait to get there. Budge up," she added to Zara. "I can't see the map properly."

The map was usually protected by a magical force field but as the teachers and students crowded into the hall it shimmered and fell away. Ms Nettles sat on her unicorn, Thyme, examining the west coast of the map and discussing with Ms Tulip, Ms Rosemary and Ms Rivers where would be the best place to make a camp. Mr Longnose, dressed as usual in a dark suit, seemed to be arguing with them.

Nudging Zara, Phoebe said, "I've just thought of something, why doesn't Mr Longnose have a unicorn?"

"He didn't come to the academy when he was

younger so he went to a different school and he's never had one," said Zara. "In fact, I heard Ms Tulip telling Ms Tansy that he can't even ride!"

"Ms Tulip won't let him get away with that if he stays much longer!" said Lily with a grin. "She thinks everyone should ride!"

"Ms Tulip is looking at him rather a lot," said Phoebe, observing the riding teacher who kept glancing at Mr Longnose. "Perhaps she's planning to get him on a unicorn while we're at the beach!"

Aisha giggled. "Or a donkey!"

Lily grinned. "Do you think he'll put on swimming shorts and go paddling in the sea while we're there?"

They all burst into giggles at the thought.

Ms Nettles raised her hand for silence. "Quiet please, everyone. This is the first time I've used the map to transport the whole school. The magic should be strong enough but for it to work,

everyone must hold hands. Don't let go or you will be left behind."

Phoebe took Zara's hand as Zara took Lily's. Phoebe was very glad she wasn't next to Mr Longnose. She definitely wouldn't want to hold hands with him!

Ms Nettles cleared her throat. "Are we all ready? Aisha, you're not holding on to anyone."

"Sorry," said Aisha, who was suddenly shrugging off her rucksack. "I think I've forgotten something important."

Ms Nettles sighed. "If it's your flute, my dear, then I can see it sticking out of your bag."

"Phew! Thanks, Ms Nettles."

Phoebe grinned and squeezed Aisha's hand as she took it. Aisha squeezed back.

Ms Nettles placed her free hand on the magical map. Speaking in a loud clear voice, she said, "Take us all to the west coast."

Phoebe and Shimmer

At first, Phoebe thought that the humming noise she could hear was Aisha but then she realised it was the magical map. A wind sprang up, snatching Phoebe's hair and whipping at her cheeks. Zara's and Aisha's hands were ripped from hers as the wind lifted Shimmer up. Lights flashed and then they were spinning so fast that it was impossible to see.

"Eeeeeee!" squealed Phoebe, grasping hold of Shimmer's mane. Her long plaits flew around her face as she spun through the air, then just as suddenly she was falling. Her stomach dipped as the ground rushed up to meet her, but Shimmer landed safely with only a soft bump.

"Wow!" said Phoebe, catching her breath as Zara, Aisha and Lily landed beside her on their unicorns. Around her, unicorns, students and teachers were landing with gentle thuds. They were on a grassy clifftop that rolled down to a cliff edge where red rocks fell away to golden sand beneath. In the distance, Phoebe could see the blue sea.

"Isn't it beautiful?" said Aisha.

"Oh, it's so good to smell the sea again!" said Lily, sniffing happily. She and her mum lived on the east coast.

There was a louder bump and a strangled shout

behind them. Phoebe turned and had to clamp her hands over her mouth to stop herself from laughing. Mr Longnose had arrived and landed face down with his legs crumpled beneath him and his bony bottom sticking up in the air. His face was berry beetle red as he scrambled up and brushed the grass from his smart, dark suit.

"Ms Nettles!" he said crossly. "You have brought us to the wrong place. I distinctly remember saying that we would camp on the beach. We shall be recording the level of the tide at all hours of the day and night and I don't want to have to walk too far."

Ms Nettles sucked in her cheeks. "Thank you, Mr Longnose, but while I am headteacher, the safety of my students is my responsibility. Given the unusual fluctuations in the tide, it would not be safe for them to camp out on the beach as their tents could easily be washed away by an

exceptionally high tide. Everyone can access the beach by one of several cliff paths." She held Mr Longnose's eye until a pink flush spread up his neck.

"Very well," he said, shortly. "You may continue to allocate the students' campsites."

Ms Nettles' mouth pursed.

Ooh, she really doesn't like him, Phoebe thought, reading her expression.

After a moment, the headteacher nodded. "The teachers will camp here then each dormitory will pitch their tents at a different site in a line along the cliffs. Amethyst dorm, you will have the campsite furthest away. Ms Rosemary, will you show them where to go please?"

"Of course," said Ms Rosemary. She patted her unicorn and smiled at the girls. "Come on then, follow me."

They rode for a while until the cliff began to

slope down and they spotted a cluster of stone houses nestled above the beach. Ms Rosemary pulled up on clifftop in a spot that was sheltered by bushes and a crumbling stone wall. "This can be your campsite. Set up your tents. I will ride down into the village and tell them you're camping here."

"Let's pitch the tents by the wall so we have some protection from the wind," said Zara, as Ms Rosemary rode away.

There were three tents. Phoebe and Zara were sharing one, Aisha and Lily were sharing another, and there was one for their things. They put them up with their backs to the wall and then made a fire of sticks, using rocks to stop it from spreading when they lit it. Ms Rosemary returned at a gallop, her face flushed.

"Girls, I need your help! The village was flooded last night after a freak high tide that came halfway up the cliff."

"But Mr Longnose said there wouldn't be flooding here," said Aisha, in surprise.

"I know but he clearly was wrong. There's quite a mess so I need you to come with me and lend a hand with the clearing up."

The girls jumped on their unicorns.

"A freak high tide that no one expected!" exclaimed Zara, as they headed towards the houses. "Another unusual environmental event." Her eyes gleamed. "There could be something suspicious about it. Keep a look out for clues, everyone!"

CHAPTER SIX

As they cantered into the village, Phoebe felt like a superhero, swooping in and coming to the villagers' rescue. However, she quickly discovered that cleaning up after a flood was not exciting in the least. The first thing that hit her was the smell coming from the piles of rotting seaweed. The doors of buildings were thrown open as people wearing welly boots shovelled it out of their houses and swept away the remaining water. There were piles of debris everywhere; soggy bedding, clothes and rugs were all tangled up with seaweed and shells and items that had been swept into the

surrounding fields by the flood.

The villagers were very pleased to have the girls' help. Lily and Feather set to work immediately, using Feather's magic to help retrieve the heaviest

items that had floated away. The other girls grabbed brooms and started to sweep out the water, while their unicorns picked things up with their teeth and hung them out to dry.

Clearing up was very dull and Phoebe soon got bored.

"I wish I'd discovered my magic," Shimmer said with a sigh as they paused to watch Feather, who was using hers to carry a cart back from the fields.

Phoebe couldn't have agreed more. Doing magic and being applauded would be much more fun than sweeping and wringing the water out of wet clothes. "How about we go to that ruined cottage on the cliff path over there? I can see some things that need retrieving and at least we'll get away from the smell for a while."

"OK," said Shimmer eagerly.

Phoebe vaulted on to his back and they cantered

across the grass. The cottage roof had fallen in a while ago and moss clung to its stone walls. Clearly, no one had lived in it for quite some time and as Phoebe and Shimmer got closer they saw that the walls were just an empty shell. The grass surrounding it was scattered with objects that had been swept there by the flood water − buckets, flowerpots, baskets...

Phoebe jumped off Shimmer and started collecting any objects she could carry. As she got close to the gaping doorway, something moved in the shadows inside the ruin. She gasped and jumped as a seagull flew up into the air with a loud cry.

Phoebe took a trembling breath. It was just a bird. She picked up some more flowerpots and returned to Shimmer. He was holding a spade in his teeth.

"Let's take this stuff back to the village," she

said. "This cottage feels creepy."

When they got back, Zara came riding up on Moonbeam. "Guess what? I've been talking to some of the villagers and a few of them mentioned seeing a stranger hanging around the village in last few days. They all remembered him for his clothes – he was dressed in a black suit with long coat tails and a tall hat. He sounds suspicious, doesn't he?"

"Ooh, yes. He could be the culprit who caused the purple tornadoes and he might be responsible for the floods," said Shimmer.

Moonbeam nodded. "It feels like someone has been doing dark magic around here. The air is thicker – heavier," she said uneasily.

"I feel it too!" said Phoebe. She couldn't actually feel anything different about the air but it was great that Moonbeam was adding to the drama and tension.

"We mustn't jump to conclusions," said Zara quickly. "We need evidence, we can't just go on vague feelings but the sighting of this man is definitely a possible clue. The villagers I spoke to said he was seen hanging around the beach and walking near the old ruined cottage."

"We've just been there," said Phoebe

"Did you see anything?" Zara asked eagerly.

"Well, it did feel creepy and I saw something move in the shadows," said Phoebe.

Shimmer nodded. "It made Phoebe jump a metre high!"

Seeing the look of enthusiasm on Zara's face, Phoebe couldn't resist adding to her story. "It might have been a person. In fact, I really think it might have been a man!"

Zara gasped. "We need to investigate this. Come on!" Moonbeam whinnied and set off for the cottage.

As Shimmer followed them, Phoebe felt a flutter of guilt. She hadn't really seen a man. She knew it had been just a bird. She hadn't thought Zara would be quite so excited.

Zara and Moonbeam went into the ruins of the cottage.

"Wait, Shimmer!" Phoebe said as he went to follow them. "Do you think I should tell Zara I was making that stuff about a man up?" she whispered.

Shimmer looked surprised. "No. Why?"

"Well, there wasn't one really, and now Zara thinks there was and—"

She was interrupted by a shout from Zara.

"Look at this!" Zara said, appearing in the entrance and waving something at them.

Phoebe and Shimmer went closer. Zara was holding a pale grey button with an unusual sheen, engraved with a two-headed serpent entwined around a strange symbol. "I found this inside. It must have come from the mystery man's clothes. Oh, this is SO exciting. It's a real clue! Well done, Phoebs! I wouldn't have found it if you hadn't spotted the man!"

"Well ... um—" Phoebe started to say.

"Beware the tall, cloaked stranger," Moonbeam said dreamily.

Zara looked round. "What?"

Moonbeam blinked. "Sorry. I don't know why I just said that."

Zara rolled her eyes. "Moonbeam, concentrate!

This is serious stuff. A suspect has been here and this button may well have come off his clothes. We should stake out this place tonight in case he's using it to cause trouble for the island. That's when he'll operate, under the cover of darkness when there's no one else about." She rushed on. "We'll need somewhere to hide." She looked around. "How about that falling-down shed? We can hide behind the walls. Let's go and tell the others! Operation Catch the Suspect is on!"

She jumped on Moonbeam and they galloped away.

Phoebe's heart plummeted. "Whoops," she said, looking at Shimmer.

"Don't worry," he said, nuzzling her. "Zara will never know you didn't really see a man."

"But I feel bad because she's so excited about it," said Phoebe. "And now we're all going on a stake-out to watch for someone I never saw, who

65

might not even be anywhere near here, instead of having fun camping!" She bit her lip. "Oh, Shimmer! What have I done?"

CHAPTER
SEVEN

It was getting late when they arrived back at the village. Everywhere was looking much tidier and Ms Rosemary sent the girls back to their camp. All Zara, Aisha and Lily talked about on the way was the mysterious man and the button. Phoebe got quieter and quieter.

When they reached the tents, the unicorns trotted back down to the beach to have a roll on the sand and a paddle in the sea. Phoebe went to the store tent to get Shimmer some sky berries for when he got back.

Lily followed her. "Are you all right, Phoebe?

You don't seem yourself."

Phoebe wondered whether to tell Lily the truth even though Shimmer thought she should just keep lying. She loved him to bits but she wasn't sure he was right this time. Teasing Zara and telling a few small stories was one thing, but letting her arrange a midnight stake-out and getting her hopes up that they were actually going to catch the man doing dark magic was quite another. She decided to confess. "I've … I've done something really stupid, Lily."

"What?" Lily asked in concern.

Taking a deep breath, Phoebe told her everything.

"Oh, Phoebe," said Lily, shaking her head.

"What should I do?" Phoebe muttered.

"You have to own up," said Lily decisively. "Zara will be cross but she'll get over it. You can't keep leading her on."

Phoebe nodded, knowing she was right. "I'd better go and tell her now."

Lily put an arm round her. "You'll feel much better once you've confessed. I'll finish up here and feed all the unicorns. You go and see Zara. Good luck!"

"Thanks." Once Phoebe made her mind up about something she liked to get on with it immediately. She went to her and Zara's tent and lifted the tent flap. Zara was inside, writing neat notes in her detective notebook, frowning in concentration.

"Um, Zara," said Phoebe, her heart beating uncomfortably fast. "Can I talk to you?"

Zara looked up. "Can it wait? I want to draw a picture of the button so we've got a record of it in case we lose it. I'm going to look to see if the man left any more clues while we're on the stake-out."

Phoebe's tummy twisted into a knot as she ducked inside "Erm, about this stake out. I need to tell you something…"

As Phoebe confessed, Zara's smile faded.

"It was all made up?" Her voice rose. "You didn't see a man there? You *lied* to me!" She threw her notebook down.

Unhappiness curled through Phoebe as she saw the hurt and disappointment in Zara's eyes. "I'm sorry."

"So, this button isn't a clue? It probably doesn't have anything to do with him!" said Zara.

"It might," Phoebe pointed out. "The villagers

did say they had seen him walking near there. It's just *I* didn't actually see him in the cottage – or at all."

"I can't believe you lied to me, Phoebe!" Zara said angrily. "Did you think it was funny, to trick me? The island is in danger. It's not a joke! I thought you really wanted to help solve the mystery."

"I do and I am sorry. I just said that stuff about the man without thinking."

"Well, maybe you *should* think in future!" Zara exclaimed. "Oh, go away!"

Phoebe backed away and the tent flap closed. She almost never cried but now she could feel tears stinging her eyes. She hated knowing she had hurt and upset one of her best friends.

She crept off to find Shimmer. He was tucking into the bucket of sky berries Lily had left for him.

"Hi, Phoebe," he said, through a mouthful of

berries. "We just had the best water fight in the sea. I'm so good at splashing, and guess what, we saw Mr Longnose down by the water. I almost got him with a big splash!" He saw her face and broke off. "What's the matter?"

"Zara is really cross with me," Phoebe confessed. "I told her that I made up the story about seeing the man."

Shimmer looked astonished. "What did you do that for?"

"I felt bad that she was planning the stake-out and everything based on what I said I saw. Now she's really angry and not talking to me."

Shimmer huffed. "Oh, she's just being silly and making a big deal out of nothing. Ignore her."

Phoebe stroked his mane but didn't say anything. It was lovely of him to be on her side but she was the one in the wrong, not Zara.

Shimmer nudged her. "Hey, should we go

to the beach? Then you can see how brilliant I am at splashing. If I stamp my hoof like this –" Shimmer struck the ground with a hoof – "POW! The water explodes everywhere!"

Phoebe caught something bright pink flicker around Shimmer's hoof. Her eyes widened. "Shimmer, what was that?"

"What?" he said.

"I saw a spark fly up. Do it again, Shimmer. Stamp your hoof!"

"Are you tricking me?" he said suspiciously.

"No!"

Shimmer half-heartedly banged his hoof on the ground, looking as if he didn't trust Phoebe.

"Harder!" she urged him.

Shimmer smacked his hoof to the floor with a bang. "Like that? Woah!" A tiny bolt of magic shot from his hoof, criss-crossing over the grass and striking a stone. CRACK! The stone shattered,

leaving a strong, sugary smell hanging in the air.

Phoebe gawped at Shimmer. "You've found your magic! Oh, Shimmer!" She flung her arms round him and then looked over at the shattered rock. "But ... what type of magic is it?"

"I don't know!" Shimmer said in shock.

He stamped his hoof again. With a crack, a bolt

of magic flew across the grass, hitting a boulder and splitting it in half.

"Wow! That's powerful!" yelped Phoebe in excitement.

Shimmer exploded a bucket next, almost soaking them both as the water cascaded out.

Phoebe squealed. "Stop it! You're going to

wreck the camp! You'd better stop practising with it, at least until we've worked out what sort of magic you've got."

"All right," said Shimmer, reluctantly. "It's is tiring. I feel exhausted now."

"Wait here. I'll go and tell the others!" Phoebe said and, buzzing with excitement, she raced back to the tents to tell her friends the news.

CHAPTER EIGHT

"Go away!" said Zara again when Phoebe stuck her head inside her tent. She was sitting cross-legged on her sleeping bag, talking to Lily and Aisha.

Phoebe still felt bad about before but Shimmer getting his magic was far more important than any argument. "Shimmer's found his magic!" she exclaimed.

"What?" said Lily.

"It's awesome!" Phoebe rushed on. "But we don't know exactly what it is. He keeps exploding things!"

"Are you joking?" Zara gave her a withering look. "Phoebe, have you seriously not learned anything today? Making stuff up just isn't funny."

"But I'm not making this up!" Phoebe protested. "Shimmer was messing around, banging his hoof on the ground, when suddenly a mini bolt of magic flew out and a stone exploded. Then he shattered a boulder – a whole boulder – and a water bucket! It was incredible."

Zara studied her hands.

"Phoebe, be honest. Is this just another of your stories?" asked Lily, her eyes meeting hers.

"No, it's the truth," insisted Phoebe. "Cross my heart and hope to die. Come and see!"

Aisha and Lily got to their feet. "Are you coming, Zara?" Lily asked.

Zara sighed. "All right, I'll come. But you'd better be telling the truth this time, Phoebe."

They trooped outside and went to Shimmer.

He'd called the other unicorns over.

"OK, everyone, are you going to watch my magic?" he said. "Stand back then, it's *very* powerful," he boasted.

With a lot of show, Shimmer brought his hoof down on the ground. Nothing happened. He tried again and all he managed to do was to dislodge a clod of turf with his hoof. The other unicorns snorted and looked at each other.

Zara exclaimed in disbelief and stomped back to her tent. "I knew it!' she called over her shoulder. "I just knew you were lying, Phoebe!"

"Phoebe!" Lily said in frustration. "I really believed you. How could you upset Zara again?"

"Wait, Zara!" Aisha called. She and Lily ran after her. Their unicorns all went too.

Phoebe fought back tears as she watched Aisha and Lily put their arms round Zara.

"Phoebe, I'm so sorry." Shimmer's eyes were

huge. "I think I must have worn myself out using my magic before, and now I've let you down and made you look like a liar in front of everyone."

"It's all right." Phoebe buried her face in Shimmer's mane so that he couldn't see how upset she was. "It's not your fault, it's mine. I do always make things up. I don't blame Zara and the others for not believing me this time." She shook her head. "I tried to change before but didn't manage it. From now on, I really am going to tell the truth. If I start exaggerating, then you must stop me and not encourage me." Phoebe looked Shimmer in the eyes. "If we're going to make good guardians of Unicorn Island then we have to bring out the best in each other, not the worst."

Shimmer nodded solemnly. "You're right, Phoebe. I love the way you tell stories and make everything so exciting but people need to be able trust us, particularly now that I have my magic, whatever it is."

"I'll help you find out. We'll start tomorrow." Phoebe cuddled up closer to Shimmer. "I love you, Shimmer. You're the best unicorn ever."

"I love you too, Phoebe," he said, nuzzling her.

Shimmer lay down and Phoebe snuggled under his mane, cuddling it like a soft silky blanket. It had been a long day and she suddenly realised how tired she was. She was just dozing off to sleep when Aisha and Lily came out to find her.

"Are you OK?" Aisha asked softly.

Phoebe nodded sleepily. "I think I'm going to sleep under the stars tonight with Shimmer."

"But you haven't had any dinner," said Aisha.

"I'm OK," said Phoebe. She didn't want to go back to camp and face Zara. "I'll have a big breakfast in the morning."

"Wait here!" said Lily. She and Aisha hurried away and came back with Phoebe's dinner of sandwiches and an apple.

"Thanks," Phoebe said.

"See you in the morning," they said.

She smiled as they crept away. At least Aisha and Lily didn't hate her. The hard knot of upset inside her began to loosen. She ate her cheese sandwiches, shared the crusts and her apple with Shimmer, then closed her eyes and seconds later she was fast asleep.

Phoebe woke at first light to the cry of seagulls as they swooped overhead. Sitting up, she ran a hand through her tangled hair.

"Morning," Shimmer whickered, his breath warm on her cheek.

"Morning," said Phoebe, stretching.

Shimmer got to his feet. "I feel much better after a good night's sleep. I've got loads of energy. I bet my magic will work again now."

Moving away from Phoebe, he stamped a hoof. Sparks fizzed up into the air and a nearby rock shattered into hundreds of pieces.

Phoebe clapped with delight. "That's awesome, Shimmer. If only we knew exactly what magic it is. I wish we could ask Zara about it. She's really good at scientific stuff like that."

"There's Zara now," said Shimmer, nodding towards the coastal path. Phoebe followed his gaze and saw Zara riding Moonbeam down towards the beach.

"I think I might go after her and try apologising again," she said.

"Let's both go," said Shimmer. Phoebe jumped on to his back and they cantered after Zara and Moonbeam. They caught them up on the beach. Zara had dismounted and both she and Moonbeam were staring out at the distant sea. It was really far out, leaving a vast expanse of bare, damp sand. Slipping from Shimmer's back, Phoebe ran over to stand beside Zara.

"Zara, I'm sorry," she said. "I really didn't mean to upset you yesterday. I shouldn't have lied about seeing the man. It was stupid of me and I'm going to try to tell the truth from now on and not make stuff up. But I wasn't lying about Shimmer, he really does have his magic."

Zara glanced at her. "Really?"

"Yes, it didn't work yesterday because he'd tired himself out. It's working again now." Phoebe flicked her hair. "I can show you—"

Zara gasped. "Phoebe! Your hair." Reaching out she lifted a long strand of pink and pale blue. "You and Shimmer have bonded!"

"We have?" Phoebe squinted to look. "Shimmer, we've bonded!" she squealed, kissing him.

"It must have happened in the night," he whickered, nuzzling her back.

"Aw! Well done, you two." Despite the argument, Zara looked really pleased for them.

"So, I guess that means you really were telling the truth? Shimmer actually *did* find his magic?"

"Yes, I did," said Shimmer. "Watch this." He flicked his hoof and a bolt of magic scorched across the beach, hitting a jagged rock that exploded. Zara's mouth dropped open.

"Wow!" she breathed. "Energy magic! That means you can create bolts or balls of pure magical energy. My great-aunt's unicorn, Thor, has energy magic. No wonder you tired yourself out yesterday when you found it. It's very powerful."

"Zara, something doesn't feel right," Moonbeam

said uneasily, staring out over the sand. "The air feels wrong."

Phoebe followed her gaze. "The sea is really far out, isn't it?"

"Yes," said Zara, her forehead crinkling. "It shouldn't be. It should be halfway in by now according to the tide times."

"It's coming," Moonbeam muttered.

"It doesn't look like it is," said Zara, giving her a puzzled look. "It looks like it's going out."

"Beware the man with the cloak," Moonbeam said.

"The man with cloak! Why are you being weird again, Moonbeam?" Zara demanded.

Moonbeam blinked. "I … I don't know. I'm sorry. I don't know what I meant."

"Hey, everyone," Shimmer interrupted. "It's gone really quiet all of a sudden. There are no birds and I can't see the sea any more."

Phoebe realised he was right. There was no sign of the sea at all now, just miles and miles of sand that rolled on as far as the eye could see. "What's happening?"

Zara's face paled. "Oh no! I've read about this. It happens before a tsunami hits."

"What's a tsunami?" said Shimmer uncertainly.

Zara gulped. "A giant tidal wave that sweeps away anything and anyone in its path!"

CHAPTER NINE

"Quick! We've got to warn the others!" Phoebe cried.

Phoebe and Zara leapt on to their unicorns and thundered back up the cliff path, yelling loudly to wake their friends up.

"What's all the noise about?" Aisha said as she and Lily stumbled from their tents, pulling on clothes.

"Phoebe! Your hair!" Lily gasped. "You've bonded with Shimmer."

"Yes, and he really does have his magic – energy magic – but that's not important right now,"

Phoebe said. "What matters is that everyone is in danger!"

The words tumbled out of Zara and Phoebe as they explained about the sea.

"What can we do?" asked Aisha.

"Nothing," said Lily, ashen-faced. "There is absolutely nothing that can stop a tsunami. The only thing to do is get as far away as possible."

"We need to warn everyone before it hits," said Phoebe frantically.

"Let's go!" said Lily.

"Wait!" cried Zara. She pointed at Lily. "There *is* something that can stop a tsunami! I read about it in one of the books last night. Scientists have a new theory. There are special types of sound waves called acoustic waves that can move really fast through the ocean, and scientists believe that if these waves of energy could be shot right into a tsunami, they could break it up and weaken it.

They haven't found a way to do it yet, it's just a theory."

"Well, how will that help us?" said Phoebe. "If the scientists don't know how to fire acoustic waves into a tsunami then what can we do?"

"Use magic!" said Zara, her eyes gleaming. "If Shimmer shoots the tsunami with pure balls of energy, it might just have the same effect as firing acoustic waves. It may break up the tsunami before it hits the coast."

"Could it work?" said Lily.

"I don't know. But it's our only chance." Zara looked at Shimmer. "Would you try, Shimmer?"

He glanced uncertainly at Phoebe. "Do you think I can do this?"

Phoebe stroked his cheek. "I think you can do anything you set your mind to."

He seemed to grow several centimetres taller. "Then I'll try!" he declared.

"You'd better be quick!" whinnied Moonbeam.

Phoebe gasped as she looked out to sea and saw a huge blue wall of water rolling towards them. It seemed to blot out half the sky. *We're doomed* she thought, but then she realised she had a very important job to do and she had to stay calm. She didn't speak her thought out loud. "You can do this, Shimmer," she told him fiercely. "I know you can."

"We believe in you, Shimmer!" cried Zara, lifting her voice above the thundering of the water.

"Try, please try!" begged Lily as their unicorns whinnied encouragement.

Shimmer reared up and stamped both front hooves on the ground as hard as he could. A massive blue ball of energy exploded from his hooves and shot through the air, towards the incoming tsunami. Phoebe held her breath as it

smashed into it.

"Again, Shimmer!" she cried.

Zara whooped. "We're combining magic and science. This is amazing! Go, Shimmer!"

Shimmer stamped his hooves over and over again. Huge balls of energy bowled through the air, hitting the tidal wave one after the other. Shimmer's sides heaved and his legs began to buckle, and still he kept on.

"The wave is slowing down!" yelled Lily. "I'm sure of it."

"Keep going!" shouted Aisha

The gigantic wave had slowed but was still approaching. The thundering was so loud, Phoebe could hardly hear herself think. Her heart thumped for the villagers who wouldn't have time to run for their lives – for her school friends on the clifftops, for the teachers and all the unicorns. Shimmer was their only hope. Her throat

tightened. "Keep trying,
Shimmer! Don't give up!"
she begged. "You can beat the wave!"

The wave peaked, cresting in a huge curl of
white froth.

It's over, thought Phoebe. But ... wait ... was
that a wobble? The giant wave teetered as if it
no longer had the strength to carry on. Gaps
appeared in its body, holes breaking through the
thick blue wall as the water splashed back into the
sea and the wave slowly shrunk.

"Fire again!" gasped Phoebe, giving Shimmer
a kiss. His body trembled with tiredness but he
cracked his hoof down on the ground, sending
the largest bolt of pure magic yet spinning into

the centre of the wave. The wave folded over as if it had been punched in its gut.

As the wave teetered, a man's voice could be heard bellowing furiously above the fading roar of the water. *"You think you can stop me but you can't. I will return, and next time, chaos will reign."*

The tsunami collapsed into the sea, shooting a jet of water into the air.

"We did it!" Shimmer panted.

The frothing sea calmed to a gentle swell. Shimmer swayed too, exhausted from using so much magic. Hearing shouts, Phoebe looked round. The teachers and other students were galloping towards them and Mr Longnose was running from the opposite direction, from the coastal path by the village.

"Is everyone safe?" asked Ms Nettles as Thyme skidded to a halt on the grass.

Behind her, all the students were yelling.

96

"Did you see that wave?"

"It was massive!"

"I thought it was going to hit us!"

"What is going on here?" yelled Mr Longnose. His face was pale and his suit was creased and sandy. "What happened to the tsunami?"

"It was Shimmer! He saved us!" cried Zara. "He's got energy magic!"

"It's thanks to Zara's science knowledge – she got Shimmer to use his magic to stop the tsunami and it worked!" gabbled Phoebe. She and Zara hugged in delight.

Mr Longnose's mouth gaped open. For once, he was lost for words.

Ms Nettles also looked completely shocked. "Shimmer stopped the tsunami?"

Zara nodded and smiled at Phoebe. "Tell everyone what happened, Phoebs!"

Phoebe beamed as everyone turned to her.

She was centre stage and this time she didn't even have to make everything up. The truth was exciting enough!

As she described their adventure, Ms Nettles' glasses rattled so hard that they almost slid off her nose. "You saved everyone!" she said. "Thank you, Shimmer, for confronting danger head on to protect your friends and our island. And thank you, Phoebe, for being there for him. He could not have conjured enough energy if he hadn't had you by his side, believing in him."

"I couldn't have done it either if my friends hadn't been there," said Phoebe, smiling round at her dorm.

Everyone surged forward to congratulate Amethyst dorm. Mr Longnose hung back awkwardly until Ms Tulip went over and helped brush his suit down, then Phoebe saw him start to smile and chat to her.

Finally, Ms Nettles shooed everyone away. "Shimmer needs to rest and the girls should, too. I declare this a day off for everyone. We will spend our time at the beach."

"What about the tsunami and the man's voice we heard? It was definitely the same one that we heard in the purple tornado," Zara said.

"Leave that to us," said Ms Nettles, firmly. "The staff will investigate the matter."

As the teachers left, Phoebe fed Shimmer handfuls of sky berries until he began to get his energy back. "I'm so proud of you!"

"I'm proud of you too," he countered. "And guess what I've learned today? Being centre stage is so much nicer when you've actually worked hard to get there, especially if you do it with a friend. Defeating the tsunami was the most difficult but best thing I've ever done. I couldn't have managed it without your help. We're great partners! We'll be guardians together for ever and that feels amazing."

Phoebe smiled. "I feel the same."

"Come on you two," Zara ran over. "Ms Nettles said we can have our breakfast on the beach. Sausages cooked on the barbecue!"

A short while later, Phoebe and the others were sitting on rugs on the sand, finishing off their sausage sandwiches while their unicorns splashed in the sea. "This is the nicest breakfast ever," Phoebe said with a contented sigh. "Food always tastes better when it's cooked and eaten outside." She looked round at her friends. "Look, I just want to apologise to you all, but especially to Zara, for telling stories. I promise not to tell a story ever again!"

"Don't do that!" Aisha was alarmed. "We all love your stories."

"Yes, don't change too much," Lily added. "We really do like you just the way you are."

Zara grinned. "Just promise me you won't make up stories about important things like suspects and clues any more, OK?"

"OK," said Phoebe. "I promise I won't do that and I promise that I'll always tell the truth when it matters." She felt a rush of happiness. Her friends were the best!

"You know, I keep thinking about that voice in the tsunami," said Lily with a shiver.

"I'll return," Phoebe mimicked in a spooky voice.

"Who is he and what's he going to do next time?" said Aisha.

"We've got to try and find out." Zara pulled the button out of her pocket. "I wonder if this *is* a clue. After all, even though you didn't see the strange man in the ruined cottage, Phoebe, the villagers said they'd seen him near there. This

could be from his clothes."

"I bet it is," said Phoebe.

They passed the button round.

"I wonder why he wants to harm the island,"
said Aisha.

"I don't know, but it's a mystery I plan to solve."
Zara's eyes shone. "Who's with me?"

"Me!" they all shouted back.

"We'll work out who the mystery man is and solve the crime!" whooped Phoebe. "Amethyst dorm are the best!"

"Look at Shimmer," said Lily suddenly. The unicorns were playing in the surf. Shimmer was stamping his hooves, sending mini bolts of magic bouncing across the water, soaking the other unicorns as the magic exploded in the waves.

"Yay! Water fight!" shouted Phoebe, jumping up and running down to the surf line. She squealed with delight as Shimmer shot a ball of energy into the water, soaking her from her head to her toes. She flung her arms round his neck. "Do you know something?"

"What?" he said.

"You're not only the best unicorn ever with the most awesome power but you are also, one hundred per cent, my best friend."

Shimmer whinnied happily.

Phoebe beamed and shouted to the others. "Come along, all of you! It's not just fun in here, it's *magic!*"

The others leapt to their feet and raced across the sands to join the unicorns in the sparkling waves.

Another MAGICAL series from Nosy Crow!